ARLO, MRS OGG
and the
DINOSAUR ZOO

ALICE HEMMING
Illustrated by KATHRYN DURST

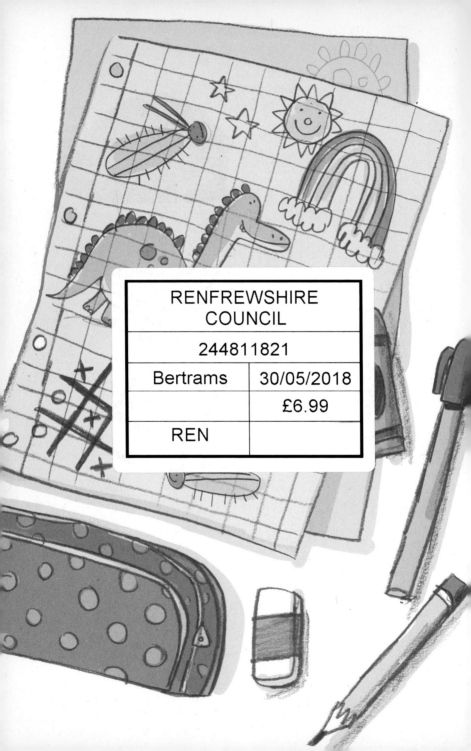

RENFREWSHIRE COUNCIL

RENFREWSHIRE COUNCIL	
244811821	
Bertrams	30/05/2018
	£6.99
REN	

My name is **ARLO** and:

1. I'm a boy. Maybe that's obvious but you never know. I once won a competition and they addressed the envelope to <u>Miss</u> Arlo Chandler.

2. I make lists. Like this one. Lists are useful. They keep everything organised and stop you forgetting stuff. I write my lists in a notebook Mum bought me at the start of the year. It has a T-Rex on the front and my name in silver letters.

ME

3. I <u>love</u> dinosaurs. I have a dinosaur duvet set, a dinosaur backpack; even dinosaur socks. I collect interesting dinosaur facts in my notebook.

4. I'm not very good with long words. I mean, I know lots of long words. I can write them. I can even say them to my friends. But if I have to speak in front of people then my words get muddled up – like mazagine and pollilop.

5. My two best friends are <u>Nathan</u> and <u>Daisy-May</u>. Nathan doesn't speak much but he laughs a lot. Daisy-May is great at drawing.

I like them both the same.

DAISY-MAY and NATHAN

Monday morning did not start well.

'Can anyone here explain to me what happened to your last teacher?' asked Ms Weebly.

It was 9.10am. At 9.10am every day, Ms Weebly liked to be in her head teacher's office with a mug of coffee and her favourite jar of pink macaroons. But not today. Today she was in our classroom faced with all of our grubby faces.

The grubby faces of class 4X.

Nobody answered. I looked at my desk and the ceiling and my fingernails. We weren't very good at keeping hold of teachers. Most classes at Purple Hill Primary were named after their teachers, like 3N (Miss Nice) and 6C (Mr Clatterbridge). But since Year 1, so many of our teachers had left that we had become class X. Then the children started leaving as well. Soon there wouldn't be any of us left.

At the front of the room, Paige shot up a hand with non-regulation pink nail polish. Ms Weebly flicked her eyes around the room, ignoring Paige.

'Nobody at all?'

I unhinged my pencil tin; keeping both hands on the lid as I prised it open so it didn't make a sound. I slid out my little blue notebook and found the right page.

4X EX-TEACHERS

1. <u>Mr Yau.</u> December 6th: Went to the stationery cupboard for glue sticks. Never came back. Ms Weebly had to teach us for the rest of the year.

2. <u>Ms Kettle.</u> January 5th: New year, new teacher, new record: didn't last a day. The twins fell out of the window, the ambulance came and she left right behind.

3. <u>Mrs Moses.</u> March 24th: Took early retirement after an incident with jelly in the sandpit. She was twenty-seven.

4. <u>Mr Austin.</u> June 30th: Ran away after Daisy-May's Show and Tell.

Ms Weebly spotted me checking my notebook. 'Any idea why Mr Austin left, Arlo?'

I knew why he left. But saying it aloud was different.

'Mr Austin, well he... I mean... It was a Wen...nesday–'

Ms Weebly sighed.

'I forgot you're the wrong child to ask if I want a quick answer,' she said.

I was sitting in between Nathan and Daisy-May. Nathan never really spoke but Daisy-May came to my rescue.

'What Arlo is trying to say, is we don't know,' she said, wrapping a springy lock of black hair around her finger.

This time, Paige started speaking before she was chosen.

'It was Daisy-May's Show and Tell, Ms Weebly. Ask anyone.'

'It was not!' Daisy-May said, leaping up to defend herself.

'Hissy and Missy are lovely cockroaches. It wasn't my fault they ran up Mr Austin's trouser leg. They were just looking for a safe place.'

'I get the idea, Daisy-May. You can sit down now.'

Daisy-May sat. 'If someone is that scared of

cockroaches then it is called a *phobia*,' she muttered, 'and we really should have been told.'

I nodded sympathetically. Daisy-May got like this around animals. She seemed to like the really unpopular ones like rats or spiders. Maybe that's why she liked Nathan and me so much: we were the unpopular ones of 4X.

Paige put up her hand again.

'My Dad says we are a lively bunch and we get bored easily,' she said.

'*Lively* is not the word I'd use,' Ms Weebly said.

I was not sure which word Ms Weebly would use. I consulted my notebook again.

January 5th: '4X are the most unruly, disobedient and unteachable class I have ever had to endure.' Mrs Kettle.

Maybe they were the sorts of words Ms Weebly meant.

'Mitchell, are you using that stapler as a *weapon*?' asked Ms Weebly.

Mitchell didn't reply.

'In fact, is that *my* stapler?'

'Yeah,' said Mitchell proudly. He had swiped it right from under her nose.

'Return it to me now and move your name to amber,' said Ms Weebly.

Purple Hill Primary ran a traffic light system for behaviour. In each class, every child had a corresponding laminated name-label, which was attached magnetically to a traffic light poster. All the strips started the day on the green light for good but could be moved to amber for warning or red for disaster. Mitchell moved his name across to amber and swaggered back to his seat with a wide smile and his thumbs up.

Something about this tickled Nathan. 'Mitchell!' he whispered to me. I was the only person at school who Nathan actually spoke to and only when he was laughing and relaxed. He laughed a squeaky laugh and his eyes went all crinkly, which made Daisy-May crack up. Then the whole class laughed and laughed.

Ms Weebly did not smile. She adjusted her glasses. 'You do realise that it is only 9.13am and already nine of your names are on amber or red? If I do not see an improvement in your behaviour by the end of term, then there will be no end-of-year party.'

Everyone groaned. The end-of-year party always sounded awesome. Ethan Plummer from 6C told us that last year there was a DISCO BOUNCE inflatable disco and he won some sweets that made his tongue turn blue. Our class *never* got to go to the end-of-year party. Not since Reception when Ms Weebly wasn't the headteacher – she was *our* teacher. Someone from our class found their way into the staffroom, filled up her macaroon jar with trifle and used the strawberries to draw a life-size portrait of Ms Weebly on the wall. Since then,

Ms Weebly always found a reason for us *not* to go.

Ms Weebly continued as if she was talking to herself. 'I need to get out of this classroom so that I can put out an advert for a new permanent teacher. There must be *someone* who has never heard of 4X. If only the supply teacher would arrive. She's late as it is.'

She turned to write on the whiteboard when a thump on the door made everyone jump.

'Come in!' called Ms Weebly.

A strange-looking character burst into the room. Her dress was made from patches of fur stitched together.

'SHE'S GOT BONES IN HER EARS,' said AJ, who was still working on his inside voice. Small white bones did indeed dangle from this new teacher's ears. Her hair didn't grow down in the normal way but stuck out sideways and was brown, grey and orange all at once, like Nathan's tortoiseshell cat.

'You must be the supply teacher from the new agency,' Ms Weebly said, looking her up and down, 'Miss, Mrs...?'

The fur-dressed person smiled a broad smile. 'Ogg,' she said.

Ms Weebly opened her mouth and looked as if she were about to say something but stopped. She probably wanted to get back to her macaroons. She shuffled her papers into a messy pile, scooped them off the desk, and stuck them under her arm.

'Well, Mrs Ogg,' she said, 'I will leave you to introduce yourself to 4X. I've got some work to be getting on with.'

Ms Weebly swept out of the room. For a few moments, Mrs Ogg stood by the board, grinning. We waited to see what she would do. She held a long stick like the one the teachers used to open the windows, but hers was gnarled and knobbly. She beat it steadily on the floor:

Darum dum dum, darum dum dum.

No teacher had ever behaved like this before. Nathan, Daisy-May and I looked sideways at one another.

'She's nuts!' Daisy-May whispered.

Mrs Ogg continued with her darum dum dums. Then, halfway through a darum, she stopped and looked at the class as if she was expecting us to do something. She waited for such a long time, I thought I'd better take action. I pulled my metal pencil tin towards me and hit it with my ruler.

Tappy tap tap, tappy tap tap.

Mrs Ogg pointed at me, whooped and shrieked. She leapt over, ruffled my hair and laughed. I had done something right. Nathan joined in with his hands: *clap clap.* It sounded pretty good.

Mrs Ogg, Nathan and I repeated the pattern a few times.

Darum dum dum.

Tappy tap tap.

Clap clap.

One by one, everyone joined in and soon, the rhythm echoed around the classroom. Daisy-May leapt to her feet and did a funny thumping dance. She lifted her knees up high and stamped her feet hard. Nathan, Daisy-May and I linked arms and the other children did the same in little groups as Mrs Ogg stomped around the room. She beckoned with a hand to follow and we made a long chain. We snaked around the tables and zigzagged between the chairs.

Darum dum dum.

Tappy tap tap.

Clap clap.

Stamp stomp bomp.

Mrs Ogg marched to the door, flung it open and, still beating out the rhythm with her stick, left the classroom.

I followed her lead and the rest of 4X followed me. In a long line, we darum dum dummed down the corridor, clap clap clapped past Ms Weebly's office, tap tap tapped through the dining room and stamp stomp bomped around the school field.

'This is weird,' Paige said.

'This is fun,' Daisy-May said.

'This is the best day ever,' I said.

When the mums and dads came at pick-up time, we ran out saying, 'I love Mrs Ogg,' and 'I hope she comes back tomorrow and darum dum dums.'

The mums and dads weren't so sure. 4X were a lively bunch. We needed a teacher with *experience*. No one knew a thing about Mrs Ogg. Where had she come from? Where had she gone to university? Paige's dad was on the Purple Hill PTA. He knew a lot of things about the school.

'I heard they are using a new agency now. Who knows where half of these new teachers trained,' he said to the other parents at drop-off time the next morning.

Over the next few days, our lessons grew even more unusual.

On Tuesday, we gathered leaves and berries from the playground. Back in the classroom, we squished them into different-coloured pastes. I found some berries that made a bluey-purply colour; Paige and Georgia made a yellow paste from flower petals. Mitchell's tub was a muddy brown and smelt strong. I hate to think what he put in there. With the pastes, we painted a mural of a landscape in the reading corner. The shorter kids like me crouched down at the bottom to paint the flowers and the taller ones painted the trees. The twins clambered on top of the bookshelves to put birds in the sky.

On Wednesday, Mrs Ogg taught us how to knock a round stone against a piece of flint until it was sharp enough to cut leaves. And on Thursday, we made a shelter at the top of the playing field using sticks, leaves and grass cuttings. While we played in and around the shelter, Mrs Ogg lit a large bonfire and crouched in front of it, watching the flames flicker.

The mums and dads were still not sure.

'Paige told me that when the school ovens broke down, Mrs Ogg made a fire in the wastepaper bin and grilled sausages,' Paige's dad whispered to a group gathered by the school gates.

But at the end of the week, when a letter came home about a school trip, the mums and dads were impressed. 'How organised,' they said, and, 'What a good idea'. Nobody had been brave enough to take our class on an outing before.

Dear Parent

Class 4X will be visiting the zoo on Monday. Full school uniform should be worn. Please don't forget:

- A packed lunch
- No more than three pounds spending money
- A T-bone steak

Thank you,

Mrs Ogg.

The letter was signed at the bottom with a big scratchy X.

'Lovely,' said my mum, and stuck the letter to the fridge with a magnet.

On Monday, the sky was full of white clouds, although the rain stayed away. Ms Weebly greeted the parents at the gates with a smile that quivered at the corners.

'*Interesting* hair decoration, Paige, but it is not proper uniform,' she said. Paige sighed dramatically, removed the red fabric flowery clip and stuffed it into her backpack.

Ms Weebly cleared her throat and glanced at her usual stack of papers.

'As you all know, 4X have never been on a school trip before because of certain *behavioural* challenges. But I have every confidence that they will behave with the maturity and manners we expect from Purple Hill Primary pupils–'

She broke off to direct a withering stare at Mitchell, who was picking his nose and wiping it down Georgia's back. He stopped mid-pick and looked at the ground. Ms Weebly continued.

'–I would have *loved* to join them on their trip but I have to be here to…erm… meet some people. About a thing. Your children will, however, be in the capable hands of Mrs Ogg.'

She gestured towards the back of the coach, where Mrs Ogg was poking a leafy stick into the coach exhaust pipe and grunting at the driver. He had a furry outfit like Mrs Ogg's and such a big scruffy beard you could hardly see his eyes and mouth. When Mrs Ogg seemed satisfied, she and the driver climbed onboard the coach and beckoned us to the steps. Ms Weebly came with us and muttered out of the corner of her mouth,

'Make sure you behave on this trip. If I receive a phone call from any one of the emergency services then there will no end-of-year party. If I receive a single complaint from the authorities at the zoo then there will be no end-of-year party. If I have to return to the zoo to retrieve any lost property, then – you guessed it – no end-of-year party.'

As we boarded the coach, we handed our shrink-wrapped steaks to Mrs Ogg, who chucked them into a cool box at her feet. Mrs Ogg crouched on the arm of the driver's seat, clicking an overhead button on and off and laughing. She wasn't assigning people partners or counting heads. She didn't seem to know all our names, let alone who was in school today. A sudden sense of doubt overwhelmed me. Could

Mrs Ogg keep us all out of trouble? If she did, then maybe Ms Weebly would let her stay as our permanent teacher. And maybe we'd get to go to the party.

Mrs Ogg needed back-up. Someone organised. Someone dependable. I looked around at the chaos on the bus. The twins were trying to squeeze into the overhead luggage racks. Mitchell was hitting AJ rhythmically around the head with his lunch bag. Naima had lost a shoe. There was only one person around here who could do the job. Me. I would keep a watchful eye and be personally responsible for ensuring no emergency services were called. Ms Weebly would not be dragged away from her macaroons. And 4X would bounce all night on the DISCO BOUNCE with blue mouths. I gulped. This would not be easy.

I sat between Nathan and Daisy-May on the
back seat. The coach rumbled as we waved
goodbye to the mums and dads on the pavement.
Nathan let me lean my notebook on his back so I
could start making notes right away.

HEAD COUNT: SEVENTEEN

Should be twenty-three but six people away:
<u>Sofia, Talisha, Yusuf and Jack</u>: off sick
(they all ate the school egg sandwiches
yesterday.)
<u>Tony Abbes</u>: Absent (I have never met Tony.
He is on the register but has never once
turned up.)
<u>Chloe Jones</u>: on holiday.

My writing went all shaky as Nathan laughed his high squeaky laugh. In amongst the laughing, he said one little word: 'zoo!'

I remembered back when Nathan and I were in nursery. We used to play with the plastic dinosaurs and he spoke all the time back then. Things like 'mine' and 'pass the stegosaurus'. He had a squeaky, high voice a bit like his laugh now. But when we started Purple Hill Primary, he stopped speaking apart from a word here or there. Ms Weebly was very scary. Maybe she scared Nathan's voice away altogether.

'Let's open our packed lunches!' said Daisy-May as soon as we'd left the school. We took a peek inside our lunch bags. Daisy-May grinned as she opened hers. She had three things for afters: some chocolate animal biscuits, a big wedge of cake and some spongy marshmallow sweets.

'The sweets are for sharing,' she said. Daisy-May always shared her stuff. As we chewed, we watched the familiar streets and houses whizz by. AJ gave a running commentary.

'MY HOUSE!'

'MY DAD'S WORK!'

'MY BIG BROTHER'S SCHOOL!'

'I have been to the zoo twenty-seven times already this year,' said Paige, re-attaching the flowery red hair decoration she had taken off for Ms Weebly. It was half the size of her head. 'I can't wait to see the baby meerkats. They are my favourites. Or the koala. He is just *so cute*. Last year my Dad sponsored him–'

Mitchell knelt up in his seat and emptied the dregs of his chocolate milk onto her hair. 'Oh no, a bird's pooed on your head,' he said as the brown streaks trickled down her blonde hair.

'Mrs Ogg! Mitchell poured chocolate milk in my hair,' shrieked Paige. But Mrs Ogg was busy looking for something in the driver's hair and she didn't seem to hear.

Georgia started singing a song that went:

'We're going to the zoo, zoo, zoo, you can come too, too, too...' and we all joined in. Daisy-May made some new words. Hers went:

'We're going to the loo, loo, loo, you can come too, too, too...'

When I had recovered from my giggling fit, I carried on with my notes.

AVOIDING EMERGENCY SERVICES

Keep an eye on

Ambulance — The twins: Pay special attention to open windows and high places.
Paige: Likely to be hit. And/Or eaten by a lion.

Police — Mitchell: Throws things. Breaks things. Takes things without asking.
AJ: Keep him away from quiet places.
Daisy-May: Might draw on something she shouldn't.

Fire — Mrs Ogg: seems to enjoy starting fires.

I gave up after that. Everyone gives up on 4X eventually.

Daisy-May had gone quiet, which normally meant she was drawing. I checked quickly to make sure she wasn't doodling on the curtains. It was ok. This time she was drawing on her arm with a blue ballpoint. Her eyes were fixed on something outside the coach. She glanced between the outside world and her arm-as-canvas, drawing long lines with her pen.

'What are you drawing?' I said, peering at the scribbles.

'Nothing,' said Daisy-May, thickening one of the lines.

'An elephant sign!' shouted Paige from across the aisle. 'That means the zoo is just around the corner!'

Three more elephant signs flashed by and then, up ahead, a brightly coloured banner with pictures of elephants, monkeys and giraffes. The zoo!

We cheered and pointed but the coach driver didn't stop. Instead, he sped up and drove straight past the entrance.

'MRS OGG,' shouted AJ, 'THE ZOO WAS BACK THERE.'

Mrs Ogg shrugged her shoulders.

'If we're not going to the zoo then where are we going?' wailed Paige.

That was a very good question but there was no answer. Mrs Ogg laughed a manic laugh and the coach driver kept on driving. Our coach left the main road and drove along smaller country roads into the hills. Then we swerved, leaving the road behind. We were heading straight for a tall but narrow crack in the rocky hillside.

'We will never fit through there,' I said to Daisy-May. The coach sped up and we hurtled straight for the hillside. I gripped the seat, eyes fixed open in horror. The gap seemed to widen as we grew nearer. Then, like a shuttle shooting into space, the coach zoomed forwards and we found ourselves in a pitch-black tunnel. In the sudden darkness there were shrieks of laughter and fear. Our faces were reflected back at us in the window like a mirror. Mitchell said 'Woooooooooo!' and everyone else joined in until we popped out into bright sunlight. The coach drove down a short stretch of road then up to a gigantic stone archway with three letters chiselled into the top:

We swung through the archway and into an empty car park.

There was no colourful sign and no pictures of giraffes.

'This doesn't look like a normal zoo,' said Daisy-May.

And I had to agree.

5.

We gathered together our bags and waterproofs and filed slowly off the coach. The cool box and lunchbags were stacked in a stone-wheeled animal skin trolley, which Mrs Ogg manoevered behind her.

'Phew, it's hot out here,' said Daisy-May. The sun had come out and the air here was like the bathroom after a shower: hot and damp.

'I'LL COOL YOU OFF,' shouted AJ, squirting his water bottle at her.

Daisy-May screamed, unscrewed the cap of her bottle and emptied the whole lot over his head.

AJ grinned and, hair dripping, looked around the dusty car park. Our coach was the only vehicle.

'WHERE IS EVERYONE?'

It was a good question. 'Maybe we're early,' I said.

There were no ticket booths, just a wall of lined-up boulders. Mrs Ogg and the driver rolled one of the smaller boulders to the side and we all squeezed through the gap.

We stood in a deserted clearing with an overgrown rocky hillside to the left and trees to the right. There were no cages. Or animals. Or even any pictures of animals. There were no monkey-shaped bins or ice cream stalls.

Paige stuck out her bottom lip. 'Great, so there are no animals, no people and just a load of dust. That's about right for 4X. We get a rubbish zoo.'

Directly in front of us was a large rock with carved arrows pointing in different directions.

Symbols, like wiggly lines for water, were
scratched below the arrows. Mrs Ogg pointed to
the boulder, with a quizzical look on her face.

One of the symbols looked like scaly skin.

'That must be the reptile house,' said Daisy-
May. 'Let's start there. Do you think they have
Komodo dragons?'

Nathan nodded excitedly. He always agreed
with Daisy-May.

'Reptiles?' said Paige, 'Like crocodiles and
snakes? Yuck! Can't we find the bears or

something cute and cuddly?'

But Mrs Ogg and the driver were already heading in the direction of the reptile arrow, talking animatedly to each other in a series of grunts and growls. We followed them up an overgrown path, winding up the rocky hillside. Something buzzed close to my ear and I darted my head out of the way. It was a dragonfly. A huge one – bright blue with clear wings.

I could hear the swish of Mrs Ogg's staff as she swept unfamiliar feathery plants out of the way. The driver bumped the trolley along behind her. We emerged, panting and wiping our foreheads. It turned out we had climbed quite high. In the hillside ahead of us was a dark cave. The reptile symbol was carved into the rock above it.

'FOUND THE REPTILE HOUSE!' said AJ.

'I think I just stepped in some poo,' said Daisy-May, wiping her shoe on the ferny carpet. We could see where her foot had squished into the steaming deposit. It was about the size of a deflated rugby ball. What creature does a poo that size? But there was no time to investigate. The rest of 4X were heading into the reptile house.

A long curtain of vines covered the cave mouth. They tickled our faces and bare arms as we pushed through. We shuffled in one after the other, onto a wobbly wooden walkway. I thought it would be cooler inside the cave but it was even hotter than out in the sun. It was gloomy too, although some light filtered through from the entrance. At the back of the cave, a gushing waterfall flowed into rocky pools on the cave floor. The walkway curved in a U-shape above the pools right into the cave and then back round towards the way we came in.

'Eurggh! This place stinks,' said Paige, holding her nose. 'Do we have to stay in here long?'

It did smell like whatever Daisy-May had just

stepped in. The walkway jiggled alarmingly under my feet and I gripped the rope strung up by the side of the path. I looked in the water but I couldn't see any reptiles.

'I might faint if it gets any hotter,' said Daisy-May. Nathan nodded, fanning himself with a leaf he'd plucked outside.

A pencil flew past my ear and landed with a splash in the pool, sending ripples to the edge of the cave. I glanced back to see who had thrown it but could only see Mitchell looking innocent. When I looked back into the murky water, a large shadow moved swiftly past.

'Do you think that was a crodo–crocodile?' I said.

Daisy-May peered in.

'It looked bigger than that and I think it had flippers.'

The creature, whatever it was, didn't swim back.

'Maybe they're all asleep,' I said.

'Or hiding from us,' added Daisy-May.

'Reptiles are rubbish,' said Paige. 'Can we go to the next bit now, Mrs Ogg?' she called.

Mrs Ogg was waiting by the exit. She nodded and made her way outside. Just then, there was a loud shriek above us, like a seagull using a loudhailer. Something flapped above our heads.

'Was that a *bat*?' said Paige.

The flapping noise got louder and a cool breeze ruffled our hair as something with giant wings swooped close to our heads. Whatever it was was much bigger than a bat.

Paige screamed first, but then everyone joined in and the whole of 4X stampeded towards the exit and burst out into the bright sunshine. That's when we saw the view.

We stood up on the hillside with our backs to the cave and the whole zoo spread out below us like a patchwork quilt. It was a mammoth place. There were some dusty areas, some lush and green. Clusters of trees were dotted around but they didn't look like the trees near us at home – they had long trunks and most of the leaves were near the top. A river ran right through the zoo, filling a large pool, and on the far side was a dark green mass of forest. I couldn't see any animals.

Mrs Ogg rummaged in her trolley and took out a round clay object the size of a satsuma. It

had a hole in the top and a short funnel. She cupped her hands around it and blew into the funnel, fanning out her hands as she did so. The sound that emerged was loud and deep like a wind instrument. It echoed all around us.

WAAAAAAAAAMP

And then, from down below, came a reply, like a distant foghorn:

WAAAAAAAAAAMP

Seventeen pairs of eyes squinted to try and see where the sound was coming from. A herd of animals emerged from behind a cluster of trees below. They were strange animals with pipes on their heads and seemed to be playing the same tune as Mrs Ogg. Not kangaroos, although they were walking on their hind legs. They made their way to the water, still hooting.

And then, where there had been emptiness, there was movement. Some heavy, spiky creatures stomped into the enclosure behind them. Tiny unfamiliar mammals scratched about in a nearby bush. And a giant winged creature swooped out of the cave mouth behind us, flapping over our heads and out into the hazy blue sky. It was not a bat. It was as big as one of us, with huge wings and a beak. I recognised it before anyone else but its name was too long to say.

'Wow!' I said. 'This is no orni...dary zoo, I mean–'

'IT'S A DINOSAUR ZOO!' shouted AJ.

7.

'Awesome,' said Mitchell. 'I want to see
those spiky dinos first.'

'No, the hooty ones,' said Daisy-May.

'I want to go home now,' said Paige.

I didn't say anything. A dinosaur zoo? But
there had been no dinosaurs on the planet for 65
million years. Maybe they were just *really*
lifelike models.

Mitchell and Daisy-May began scrambling
down the path we had just climbed but Mrs Ogg
clapped her hands and guided us back nearer the
cave. Just by the entrance was a metre-wide
hole in the ground. Mrs Ogg beckoned, and

opened her hand towards the hole, invitingly. But none of 4X seemed keen.

'She has got to be joking,' said Daisy-May.

Mrs Ogg looked impatient. She grabbed the driver's arm. He looked a little startled, but it was hard to tell what was going on under that beard. He sat with his legs dangling in the hole and Mrs Ogg pushed him.

AAAAAaaaaaaaaah!

His head and shoulders disappeared into the hole.

'IT'S A SLIDE!' shouted AJ and everyone rushed to be the first down. This was a disaster waiting to happen. There could be a mid-slide pile-up. I remembered when I was on holiday there was a lifeguard at the top telling people when to go.

'Mrs Ogg, can I tell people when it's safe to go?' I asked. She nodded, so I stood by the hole. I counted one-dinosaur, two-dinosaur, three-dinosaur in my head and gestured when it was each person's turn. Nathan was the last in the queue and turned to smile at me before he slid down. Then it was my turn. Was it a steep drop? Mrs Ogg didn't give me much time to think about it. She helped me sit down, gave me a quick pat that was almost a shove, and I was off.

The slide was not quite as scary I had feared. I sped round the twists and turns, catching up

with Nathan just before the end. We shot out
into the daylight and I pretty much landed on top
of him in a giggling heap. 'Fast!' he said, in
amongst his giggles.

As we sat there laughing, Daisy-May turned
to us, finger on her lips.

'What is it, Daisy-May?' I said, getting to my
feet. The slide had deposited us in front of a low
wall enclosing some dusty beige ground and
four stocky trees. I followed Daisy-May's gaze
to the tree trunks. They were more green than
brown with an unusual scaly pattern. Halfway
up each one was a round knothole that looked
very much like a baggy knee.

As I stared, the four trees took it in turns to
bend and move to the left.

'Legs!' I said aloud. I looked further up to
the gigantic body, the curving tail and the long,
graceful neck with its tiny head.

'Dinosaur legs!' I whispered. From close up,
there was no question: these were not models.

Mrs Ogg emerged from the slide and stood in front of the wall, grinning proudly. Nobody said a thing. Not even AJ. The sheer size of the dinosaurs took a while to process. They were *huge*. Each dinosaur could probably take out the whole of 4X with a single swish of its long tail.

Nathan tapped me on the shoulder.

'What, Nathan?' I said, not wanting to drag my eyes away from the spectacular sight before me. I knew Nathan wanted to know what type of dinosaur it was.

'I think this is the Atap–Apat–Asat–' I said, looking for the name in my notebook.

'Apatosaurus?' said Daisy-May, reading over my shoulder.

'Yes,' I said in a whisper.

Shorter than the Diplodocus. Previously known as a Brontosaurus. An adult Apatosaurus is around 21m long – about as long as two-and-a-half London buses.

But these dinosaurs were only about as long as one bus.

'Maybe they aren't fully grown yet,' I whispered.

The sound of running water from the other side of the wall drew my attention. A waterfall gushed out from between the legs of the Apatosaurus.

'HE'S DOING A WEE!' shouted AJ in what was most definitely his outside voice, pointing delightedly over the fence. The unending torrent continued splashing onto the ground as we all pointed and laughed. Nathan was laughing so much he held onto the fence to stop himself collapsing on the floor. 'Wee wee,' he squeaked to me.

Despite the noise, I heard another smaller trickle of water to my left and noticed a puddle spreading beneath Naima's feet. I'm not sure whether the excitement of the day or the sound of running water was to blame. AJ also noticed.

'NAIMA'S DONE A WEE TOO!' he yelled, but nobody reacted; the dinosaurs were much more interesting. Naima approached Mrs Ogg. Naima couldn't speak much English but her shuffling from foot to foot alerted Mrs Ogg to the situation. Mrs Ogg greeted the news with a smile and a shrug.

'New trouser?' said Naima.

Mrs Ogg scratched her head, nodded and smiled again, before ushering Naima behind a nearby tree with her trolley. Without Mrs Ogg, the 4X volume grew even louder. Mitchell threw a handful of gravel over the low wall. It hit the smallest dinosaur just below the knee and bounced off. This didn't seem to be a very good idea. Wouldn't it make the dinosaur cross? Mrs Ogg wasn't there to tell him. I looked around for the driver. He was slumped with his back to the wall and his eyes closed. He didn't look as though he was going to take control.

'It doesn't seem like a good idea to throw

those stones…' I tried, but Mitchell either didn't hear or completely ignored me. The twins shinned up a gnarly tree to get a better look at the dinosaur heads. Ollie swung upside down by his knees on a low branch, while Molly headed for the upper branches.

'OI, PINHEAD!' shouted AJ, jumping and waving his arms at the smallest dinosaur. It may have been AJ's ear-splitting voice or a late reaction to the gravel attack but the dinosaur seemed to suddenly become aware of our presence and swung its gaze around to look at us. Then it took a couple of great lumbering steps towards us.

STOMP, STOMP.

The fence and the nearby foliage quivered under its weight. 4X all shouted and screamed, apart from me. I covered my ears. The curious dinosaur lowered his head towards the group; towards Paige in particular. Paige stood rigid,

her face pale, as the dinosaur's great neck
stretched in front of her and looked back round,
still chewing. The piercing screams all around
didn't seem to bother the pinheaded dinosaur in
any way. A prickle of fear ran up my spine as
AJ put into words what we were all thinking:

'THAT DINO IS GOING TO EAT PAIGE!'

I did a quick risk assessment. The twins were in danger of falling three metres out of the tree. They might get away with bumps and bruises if they were lucky, but Ms Weebly would almost certainly cancel the party if an Apatosaurus ate Paige.

I made my decision, leaped forward and pushed Paige to the ground just as the huge beast delicately plucked the flowery hair decoration from the top of her head.

'Thank you, oh thank you,' she cried dramatically, looking as though she might faint.

Nathan giggled again.

'What, Nathan?' I said.

He took my book and pointed to my facts page.

The Apatosaurus is a herbivore.

'Of course, they are hervi–herbibo–they only eat plants,' I said, embarrassed.

The Apatosaurus seemed unimpressed with the fabric petals and spat out a soggy, partially chewed hair decoration. He lumbered back towards his herd, no doubt searching for more interesting snacks.

Paige looked disappointed.

'I was in real danger,' she protested as the rest of 4X shrieked with laughter. I flicked back to the emergency services page of my notebook:

Paige: Most likely to get eaten by a ~~lion~~ dinosaur

Paige stood next to me and put a hand on my

shoulder.

'You were so brave!' she said.

Brave? No one had ever called me brave before. I edged away as she was standing a bit too close but still, I felt a tiny bit taller at that word.

'Thanks,' I mumbled.

Mrs Ogg and Naima reappeared from behind the fence, Naima wearing a smaller version of Mrs Ogg's furry dress. She looked delighted and seemed to have developed a Mrs Ogg style walk, head hanging forward, arms swinging.

Paige humphed. 'So unfair,' she muttered. 'We all have to wear proper uniform apart from Naima.' She set about adapting her uniform to the heat. She tucked the bottom part of her school polo shirt back on itself and out through the neck so it was a crop top and rolled her knee socks right down. Mitchell looked impressed. He took off his polo shirt and wrapped it round his head like a bandana. Daisy-May whipped a

ballpoint pen out of her hair and drew a cool
tattoo-style dinosaur skeleton on my arm. I was
keen to get out of this place before 4X got into
any more trouble.

'Where next?' I said.

9.

'Where next' turned out to be a large rock pool. It was the size of the school hall and surrounded by piled-up boulders, arranged like deep stairs around the edges. The water was murky beige with an oily sheen on the surface. We sat on one side, near a cluster of trees that looked a bit like Christmas trees on long stalks. They provided welcome shade from the glaring sun. There was absolutely nothing in the pool. Not a ripple or a flicker of a fin.

A restless wriggle began in the watching crowd. Mitchell and AJ zipped their waterproofs over their heads and stuck out their arms like wings.

'I'M A PTERODACTYL – EEEEEEK!' shrieked AJ.

'I just twisted my finger,' moaned Paige.

'I'm hungry,' said a voice above my head. It was Olly, only his legs swinging just in sight from a tree behind us.

I sat right by the edge, in case anyone looked in danger of falling in. Daisy-May and Nathan were on my left. Daisy-May was doodling on her knee. To my right sat Mrs Ogg, who was staring at a line of ants marching towards her. She squashed them one at a time with her finger and popped them into her mouth as if she was getting the bits of crisps from the bottom of the bag. Yuck.

'WHAT EXACTLY ARE WE WAITING FOR?' yelled AJ.

'Maybe it's a dolphin display,' said Paige, clapping her hands together.

Daisy-May stopped doodling and frowned at

Paige.

'Unbelievable. A ten-foot lizard nearly eats her and she still thinks there's some cute animal in the pool. More likely it's a giant Kraken lurking in the depths that's going to swallow us in one gulp.'

Daisy-May smiled at the thought and went back to her knee-doodle, adding multiple tentacle-covered legs.

Daisy-May had a point. Something must be lurking in that pool, otherwise why would we be sitting here? I did another risk assessment. The twins were huddled in the trees but not too high. Paige was away from the edge, so if there was something lurking, it was unlikely to eat her first. I checked my list of people to watch. Mitchell had been relatively quiet so far. At the moment he was tapping a stone against some flint to make a pointy diamond shape.

Mrs Ogg moved away from the ants and busied herself removing the furry cover from her strange, wheeled trolley. Molly threw a large branch down from the tree, narrowly missing our heads. Mitchell grabbed the stick before anyone else could and poked it into the murky waters. Was he leaning out too far? A cluster of little bubbles appeared near where he was poking. Something was breathing in there.

Mrs Ogg finished rummaging in the fur skin trolley. She lifted out a colourful tower of lunchboxes and bags and placed them on the ground next to her.

'It must be time for lunch,' said Olly.

I was surprised. Even though a lot had happened already today it couldn't have been past eleven o'clock. Lunchtime was much later.

Mrs Ogg picked the first lunchbox off the pile. It was made of hard, dark-blue plastic and had a green T-Rex on the lid.

'Yes! That's mine!' shouted Olly, elbowing

Molly out of the way as he began to climb down the tree for his lunch. But Mrs Ogg pulled off the lid, turned it upside down over the pool and shook the contents into the water. Ham sandwiches, cheese strings and a lone jammie dodger bobbed about on the surface of the pool. Olly stopped, mouth wide, and then slowly shinned back up the tree to be comforted by Molly.

Mrs Ogg peered into the water for a few seconds and when nothing happened, she moved onto the next packed lunch, threw the contents into the pool, waited and picked up the next one. Daisy-May shrugged at Nathan and me.

'We ate most of ours on the coach anyway,' she said. 'She can chuck my box of raisins in if she wants.'

Nathan nodded in agreement.

'Don't throw my lunch in!' yelled Paige. 'Mummy packed me a smoked salmon and cucumber bagel. That is the only flavour I like—'

Mrs Ogg stopped suddenly. She ran
her hand up and down the pile of lunchboxes
and Paige looked relieved.

'Yes, that's mine – the fuchsia one with the
glittery pony on the lid,' said Paige.

Mrs Ogg smiled, unzipped the pink plasticky
lunchbag and took out the smoked salmon bagel.
Paige stretched out her hand but, instead of
passing her the bagel, Mrs Ogg drew back her
hand and threw the bagel high up into the air
above the pool. The bagel curved in a graceful
arc into the water. In seconds, the cucumber
floated back to the surface but the fish and bread
had gone.

'Well!' said Paige, 'those bagels come from–'

But a shout from Georgia interrupted her.

'Look, Ronnie's up there!' she said, pointing
to some rocks on the far side of the pool.

'AND HE'S GOT NO CLOTHES ON!' said
AJ.

Ronnie? RONNIE was streaking on the rocks? I scanned the list of potential troublemakers in my notebook. Ronnie wasn't anywhere on the list. In fact, I'd forgotten he was even in 4X. But there he was, standing on the uppermost rocks on the other side of the pool, wearing nothing but a pair of FRIDAY pants. And it was Monday. His white, freckled arms were stretched above his head and his red hair shone in the sun like flames.

Then I remembered; Ronnie was not a great swimmer. He was in my group for swimming lessons in the little pool for a while. He got

kicked out for some reason but I couldn't remember why.

I flicked frantically through my notebook.

4X SWIMMING LESSONS

Date: Wednesday 15th March

Place: Purple Hill Public Pool

'Getting better' group: Me, Nathan, Daisy-May and Ronnie.✳

✳ Ronnie kept jumping in when he wasn't supposed to. He nearly <u>drowned</u> in the deep end so Ms Weebly fished him out and made him sit on the side with a book.

That's right. Ronnie was not a great swimmer but he loved jumping and diving. And there he was stretching up on his toes right on the edge of those rocks. He could drown if he jumped in there. Paige was obviously having similar thoughts. She turned her pleading blue eyes towards me.

'You have to do something, Arlo. Save Ronnie like you saved me!'

Paige was right. I shouted, 'Ronnie, don't–', but he wasn't looking at me – he was looking at Mrs Ogg. He took another step towards the edge.

'He is not water cofni–codfi–he can't swim!' I shouted but Mrs Ogg smiled and gave a single encouraging nod in Ronnie's direction. Ronnie dived into the pool, making barely a splash as he entered the water. For someone who couldn't swim, he did a great impression of an Olympic champion.

Someone had to help Ronnie. And I was brave, wasn't I? Trying not to look too closely at the water, I took off my shoes, clambered over the rocks, took a deep breath and jumped into the pool.

The water was shockingly cold and my school uniform weighed me down. I shivered as I adjusted to the temperature and grabbed Olly's empty lunchbox off the side to use as a float. Up close, the pool didn't look as dirty as it did from the outside. It even smelled ok: weedy and fishy but not yucky. I blinked the water out of my eyes. I swam uncertainly towards the middle of the pool, holding onto the lunchbox and kicking my legs behind me. I counted in my head: 1-2-3… Ronnie didn't appear. He should have popped up straight away, shouldn't he?

My heart beat fast. I took a deep breath, put my head under the water and opened my eyes. I couldn't see a thing. I lifted my head out again and looked out to the poolside for some support. Mrs Ogg and the driver were eyeing the pool but they looked much more relaxed than I felt. Mrs Ogg blew a single, highish note on her clay pipe,

Weeeeeeeeeeee

Some ripples appeared on the surface of the water. Then,

A great wave carried me backwards and a
magnificent creature burst through the surface of
the water. It was a beautiful beast. Sleek, dark
blue, and the size and shape of a dolphin but
with a much longer nose and huge round eyes.
And riding on its back, looking as comfortable
as if he were on the carousel at the fair, was
Ronnie.

Paige's look of horror turned to one of
delight. 'It *is* a dolphin display! Kind of.' She

rushed forward to get a better look. The rest of 4X rushed with her. The creature swam near the surface of the water, lashing its tail from side to side like a fish. Ronnie waved.

'An Ithy–an Icky–!' I shouted. 'It's an Ichthyosaur!' Mrs Ogg heard me and put her thumbs up but the rest of 4X were otherwise occupied. The appearance of a real-life water creature had triggered a lunchbox unzipping frenzy. Everyone chucked in their own sandwiches and soon the pool was swarming with creatures. Some were small and fish-like. Others looked like turtles with patterned shells. One or two had long necks and seal-like flippers. They snapped and nibbled at the tuna sandwiches and prawn cocktail crisps but didn't touch the cheese strings.

There was no jumping through hoops or balancing balls on noses, but the creatures did put on a show for their audience. They glided through the water and swooped over one another's backs in a synchronised display.

I felt rather foolish bobbing up and down amongst the soggy sandwiches. I kicked my way to the edge of the pool and dragged myself back out onto the rocks. There was a giant SPLASH! Olly had jumped, fully-clothed into the pool from one of the overhanging branches.

'YAY!' cheered the rest of 4X. Molly followed close behind and everyone else followed. There was shrieking, splashing and throwing of mushy snacks as 4X enjoyed their impromptu pool party. The strange swimming creatures disappeared back down into the depths.

In the middle of it all was Ronnie, floating perfectly on his back under the watchful gaze of Mrs Ogg. He gently kicked his feet and moved his hands like Ichthyosaur flippers. Somehow, in the middle of all this chaos, he was learning to swim.

I sat back down between Mrs Ogg and the

driver, and attempted to wring my school shorts dry while still wearing them. I couldn't help but worry. 4X had just had two narrow escapes. I hadn't even considered a water-based emergency. I had only listed the top three emergency services. I went back to the table in my book to add some more.

* Lifeboats
* Cave rescue
* Bomb disposal

I felt the urge to be somewhere quiet and calm, like a library. Thankfully, Mrs Ogg clapped her hands for everyone to get out of the pool. It took some time but, after some hair-wringing, we gathered our stuff together and left the area. We wove through the trees and back out onto the dusty pathway, drip-drying in the hot sun.

As we emerged, the dinosaurs scuttled away

to their hiding places, and birds flew off their branches. Were they hiding from us? Or from something else?

A loud cry broke the silence.

GRR-Eek!

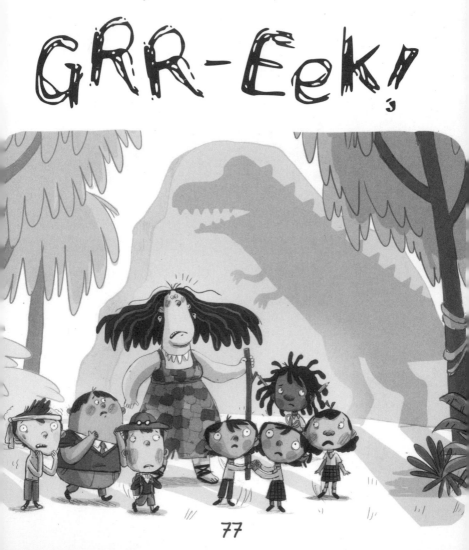

GRR-Eek!

The cry had a strange effect on me, like a fork scraping across a plate. All the little hairs on my arms stood on end. I knew instantly that I did not want to meet whatever was making that sound.

A large dinosaur with a dark green scaly body, a feathery tail and rows of sharp teeth stamped slowly towards us and leant its head over the low wall. Mrs Ogg smiled in a 'how cute' way, as if a kitten had just walked in our

direction. But this was no kitten. This dinosaur
was about twice my height and longer than my
bed at home. Mrs Ogg ran her hand lightly
down its back. It lowered its huge head and its
yellow eyes checked us out. Something about
the dinosaur looked very familiar. I thought of
the picture on my notebook and Olly's lunchbox.
This dinosaur had the same muscly legs and
ridiculously short arms.

'Is it a Tynara–Tyranna–' I asked.

'A Tyrannasaurus Rex?' interrupted Mitchell.
'Can't be. It's got feathers.'

'I think he's just a toddler, like the
Apatosaurus. That's why he's still got feathers,'
said Daisy-May.

Mrs Ogg nodded. I gulped. I had never seen
a toddler that size, towering above me with razor
sharp teeth. The driver reached into the cool
box in Mrs Ogg's trolley and brought out a steak
which the T-Rex snatched straight out of his
hand. It worked its powerful jaws and I heard

crunching. I shuddered. This dinosaur was most definitely a carnivore. A carnivore I wouldn't want to upset.

'Erm, shouldn't he be in en-losure, enclover... I mean locked up?' I asked, looking at the low wall. Daisy-May rolled her eyes.

'Mrs Ogg has them all trained. They all seem to be little dinosaurs here,' she said, joining Mrs Ogg by the T-Rex. 'Have they lost their mums?' Mrs Ogg nodded again and Daisy-May gave him a gentle pat.

'Can I feed him?' she asked.

The driver passed her a couple of slabs of meat, which she fed to the scaly toddler. Daisy-May didn't seem put off by the triangular teeth so close to her hand. The rest of us waited at a safe distance. The swimming had worn us

all out. Even Mitchell was standing quietly, just fiddling with something in Mrs Ogg's trolley.

We didn't stay long. Mrs Ogg seemed eager to move us all on. I wasn't sad to wave goodbye to that particular dinosaur. Mrs Ogg led the way. Nathan, Daisy-May and I were near the back. Mitchell was the only one behind us. He threw something up and down as he walked.

'What's that?' I asked him. But, as he grinned and uncurled his hand to show me, I already knew. Mrs Ogg's special whistle. Once again, I had stopped paying attention and things had gone wrong. I should have known that he would take something out of Mrs Ogg's trolley. Mitchell raised the pipe to his lips. I stretched out my hand to stop him.

'Erm, Mitchell, I don't think that's a good–'

But Mitchell turned away from me and blew hard into the whistle. The sound that came out was nothing like Mrs Ogg's lovely musical sounds.

EEEEEEEEE!

The hideous screeching sound made us all put our hands over our ears.

Mrs Ogg, a few metres ahead of us, turned around with a look of alarm on her face. She patted her hands down her furry outfit as if looking for something.

A crash alerted us to the fact that the T-Rex toddler was smashing its way through the wall, the stones giving way as easily as building blocks.

STOMP, STOMP, STOMP.

The dinosaur took about six steps in our direction and stood so close that I could feel its damp breath. It opened its mouth inches from Mitchell's face and let out a low raspy growl, making Mitchell's makeshift bandana quiver. Mitchell stood rooted to the spot but trembled all over.

Time slowed down.

'T-REX ON THE LOOSE!' shouted AJ.

Paige and her friends screamed at the top of their lungs. The twins started climbing the nearest tree. Naima threw herself at Mrs Ogg.

The dinosaur thrashed its head from side to side still making a terrifying growling sound. There was no time to take out my notebook but I ran through my T-Rex facts in my brain. They could run at about 20mph so running away was out of the question. It was a myth that a T-Rex couldn't see you if you stood still. Mitchell could become lunch whatever we did.

The T-Rex was clearly unsettled and our noise was making it worse.

I turned slowly around to the side to face the others while keeping an eye on the dinosaur. I clapped my hands three times and said a short, loud, 'Shhh!' to 4X. Amazingly, everyone shushed. The dinosaur stopped thrashing its head. My mouth was dry but I spoke in a low, steady voice.

'Everyone stay where you are. You are us-petting – upsetting the T-Rex.' Everyone stopped. The dinosaur stopped growling, although it kept its eyes firmly on Mitchell.

'Now, don't move, Mitchell,' I said. 'Everyone else, walk slowly away.'

They all moved back apart from Daisy-May, who took a tentative step towards the dinosaur. She put out a hand to stroke its back, as Mrs Ogg had done earlier. Something about her presence seemed to soothe the dinosaur and it hung its head in a more peaceful manner.

The driver and Mrs Ogg managed to prise Naima away and pushed their way gently past the children. The driver offered the dinosaur more meat from the cool box and ushered it back to its field. Then he began work on fixing the wall by piling the rocks back in place.

Mrs Ogg smiled at me and Daisy-May and patted us both on the backs. Then she turned to Mitchell, hands on hips and said one stern, 'Ogg.' He immediately handed her back her whistle. Something made me think that he wouldn't be taking stuff that didn't belong to him for a while.

GRRRRR, GRRRR.

There was another growl. My eyes darted around in panic.

'Mrs Ogg, are you sure that T-Rex is safe now?'

'That wasn't a T-Rex,' moaned Olly. 'That was my tummy; I'm starving.'

'Me too,' I said. I hadn't eaten since the coach, which was ages ago. And all our lunches ended up in the pool.

'When I'm at the zoo with my family, we

always stop for a cheeky monkey meal at the café. We get a milkshake, burger and fries,' said Paige. 'Can I sit next to you at lunchtime, Arlo? I feel safe with you around.'

Daisy-May rolled her eyes.

'Arlo's sitting with me and Nathan,' she said.

Mrs Ogg, who was leading the procession of children with long and determined strides, kept walking. She obviously knew where she wanted to go. We nearly had to run to keep up.

'Where are we going?' asked Mitchell.

Mrs Ogg didn't answer. She pointed over a wall to our right at a group of smallish brown dinosaurs about the size of Labradors, scratching about in the dust. If we'd have seen them at the start of the day they might have been interesting but, after the cool dinosaurs we'd seen earlier, these ones looked like boring old lizards.

I had a feeling that they might be more interesting than they looked.

'Mrs Ogg, are they the ones with the long

names?' I said.

Mrs Ogg nodded and I flipped open my book. 'It's the longest one ever – look.'

Micropachycephalosaurus

I laughed. 'Mipo... Microc... I could never say that.'

Mrs Ogg didn't slow down but she turned to me and nodded her head. Then, as she walked, she beat out a rhythm with her stick just like she did on her first day:

Dum dum darum dumdumdum dum dum.

This time, Nathan was the first one to join in with his claps. He clapped the first couple of beats and I joined in with my tapping.

Clap clap darum tappy tap stomp stomp.

'Micro,' said Daisy-May, to Nathan's claps.

'Pach-y,' said Paige, to Mrs Ogg's darums.

'Cephela,' I said, tapping along.

'SAURUS,' yelled AJ, stomping.

Mrs Ogg, still stamping, raised her hands in an upward gesture.

'MICROPACHYCEPHALASAURUS,'

We all shouted together.
We stamped along to the beat.
'Micro-pach-y-cephela-SAURUS.'
'Micro-pach-y-cephela-SAURUS.'
When we shouted it all together it was hard

to tell if I was saying it right or wrong. We darum-dum-dummed along the dusty walkways and crossed a bridge over the river. There, backing onto the woods, was a large circle of flat-topped rocks around the smouldering remains of a fire. A picnic area!

Mrs Ogg strode straight towards the fire. She rummaged in her trolley, found the cool box full of meat and threw the remaining steaks into the embers one at a time. Then she used her multipurpose stick to poke at the meat. She looked right at home.

While lunch was cooking, everyone else found a job to do. Some went off with the driver and came back with armfuls of logs for the fire. He directed Olly and Molly up a palm tree to grab as many leaves as possible.

AJ and Mitchell headed straight to the river. AJ splashed to disturb the fish and Mitchell stabbed frantically with his homemade spear. It only took him a few minutes to catch one. He brought it back to the group and everyone crowded round to admire the catch. He gave a small smile and shuffled from foot to foot. I had seen Mitchell look many different ways – secretive, aggressive, defiant, even petrified in front of a T-Rex – but I'd never seen him look like this. He looked as though he cared what people thought. At the other end of the stream, Ronnie stripped back down to his FRIDAY pants and floated on his back, enjoying the sunshine.

Even Paige loosened up a bit. She picked flowers and wound them together to make a kind of crown. It looked much better than the fake flower the Apatosaurus had spat out. Georgia and Naima and their other friends followed suit.

The delicious smell of cooking drew us back to Mrs Ogg. I was ravenous. We sat in a circle around the remains of the fire. Mrs Ogg handed us each a large portion of meat on a plate made from the palm leaves. Daisy-May raised an unimpressed eyebrow.

'I can't eat that, Miss. I'm vegetarian,' she said. But Mrs Ogg had thought of that. She passed Daisy-May, Naima and some of the other kids some kind of veggie burger made from squished up mushrooms.

'Is that ok?' I asked her but it obviously was because her mouth was too full to answer. I dug into my meal in the same way. It was better than any barbecue I'd ever had. I ate every morsel of meat and licked my fingers clean.

As the slower eaters finished off their lunch, Mrs Ogg brought some drums out of her bottomless trolley. They seemed to be made of skins stretched over hollow tree trunks. She began a gentle drumming.

Dumdumdumdumdumdum.

Nathan and I joined in with our tapping.

This time, Mrs Ogg sang along to the beat. It went something like,

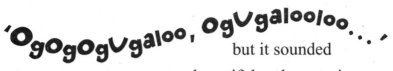
'OgOgOgUgaloo, OgUgalooloo...' but it sounded
beautiful and mysterious.

We all joined in one way or another, tapping
or singing with whatever words we fancied.
One clear voice rang out above the others. It

was Naima. Mrs Ogg smiled at her and raised her hand to encourage her to sing louder. The rest of us hushed a little so we could hear her better. I couldn't understand the words – they may have been made-up – but she sounded like a songbird. I didn't know Naima could sing. I don't think even Naima knew she could sing. And as I looked around at all the smiling faces, I wondered who else was hiding a hidden talent.

After lunch, most of 4X headed to the woods for climbing and rope-swinging fun. Nathan, Daisy-May and I found our own quiet spot behind a large rock.

'Look, there's something written here,' said Daisy-May, showing us some writing on the rock.

The bad kids at
Tweedside Primary
came here May 29th.

4J woz ere -
the worst class at
St Stephen's
if not the world

'Mrs Ogg must have taken other classes here,' I said.

Underneath, Daisy-May painted a group portrait of 4X using squished berries like Mrs Ogg had shown us. Nathan helped mash up the pastes. Underneath, she wrote:

4X. Purple Hill Primary.
Unruly, disobedient and unteachable :)

It was funny, I always thought we were the worst class in the world, but today I wondered if that were true. I made some notes.

4X HIDDEN TALENTS

Naima – singing
Ronnie – swimming/diving

96

Mitchell – hunting
Daisy-May – dinosaur training
Paige – fashion designing
Me – ??

I started to think that maybe 4X was not all bad after all. Maybe we just hadn't all found our hidden skills yet.

Mrs Ogg banged her stick on the ground and cupped her hand around her mouth.

'OGAWEEE, OGAWOOO, UGUG UG UG!' she shouted. A great flock of birds made their escape from a nearby tree and the twins poked their heads out from its leafy branches. Even Mitchell put down his spear.

Daisy-May looked up from her rock painting.

'What is she on about?'

Mrs Ogg was waving both arms in a scooping motion to gather up the whole of 4X.

'I think she's telling us it's tome hime…
home time,' I said.

I didn't want to go home. I don't think
anyone did. Apart from the almost drowning
incident and the near-miss with the carnivorous
dinosaur, it had been a perfect day.

Paige's face reverted to its usual moody
expression.

'It's *miles* back to the car park and it's hot. If
we have to walk all that way then we will
probably get dehydrated and my dad says–'

Mrs Ogg banged her stick on the ground and
Paige trailed off. Mrs Ogg put her fingers in her
mouth and whistled. After a moment's silence, a
loud thundering sound came from the woods and

a herd of animals tramped towards us. They looked a lot like elephants but with shaggy fur, long curly tusks and mischievous glints in their eyes.

'ARE THEY WOOLLY MAMMOTHS?' asked AJ.

I shook my head. 'They can't be. Mammoths lived years after the dinos. Even Mados–Masto–dons were 35 million years after.'

'Who said it is just dinos at the zoo? They're all different types of extinct animals,' said Daisy-May.

'Whatever. They look like mammoths to me,' said Mitchell.

Mrs Ogg nodded and then laughed as the beast at the front lumbered up to us and wrapped its thick trunk around AJ's waist.

'AAAARGH,' shouted AJ as the mammoth manoeuvred him, by trunk, onto its back. AJ clutched desperately onto handfuls of fur, wobbled uncertainly, then a large grin spread across his face.

'IT'S AWESOME UP HERE!'

Mitchell pushed his way closer.

'Me next! Please, please!' he begged. The mammoth plonked Mitchell behind AJ and the twins next. It tramped off, with the twins attempting to stand up on its back. Then the next mammoth took its place. Each mammoth took three or four children until just Daisy-May, Nathan and I were left. A much smaller beast (that was still enormous) shuffled over in our direction.

'Ah, we've got the little one. Isn't he adorable?' said Daisy-May.

I knew better than to say it, but the mammoth was not adorable. The mammoth's long brown fur was matted and stringy. Flies buzzed around its tail. Its trunk was not long enough to lift us, so Mrs Ogg gave us a hand

up. She put Daisy-May by its ears, then me,
then Nathan. She patted the mammoth and it
waddled forwards. I had a pony ride once on
holiday but this ride felt much higher and much
less safe. I was just attempting to get used to the
swaying motion when from a few metres ahead
came an,

'OGGUGGAWOG-UG!'

It was Mrs Ogg and the driver, shouting at
the top of their voices. They were sitting on top
of the wheeled trolley, which they'd strapped to
AJ's mammoth at the front. The mammoths
obviously understood the call because they
instantly took off at running pace. If I was
unsteady before, then now I was in real fear for
my life. I clung to Daisy-May, who seemed a
natural mammoth rider.

'Woo hoo!' she shouted from the front as we bumped and lurched along. Nathan grabbed my backpack from behind. All I could see, apart from Daisy-May's mass of curls, was a giant dust cloud and the flapping ears of the mammoths in front, who were racing one another. Thankfully, our mammoth was a lot slower than the others but even so, the journey that took ages on foot was over in minutes. The coach was a welcome sight. We came to a sudden halt and my heart rate began to return to normal.

'The other mammoths are being mean to our one,' said Daisy-May. 'They left him behind.'

Nathan and I exchanged eye rolls. We'd lost her now.

'He's got a soft bit here,' said Daisy-May, scratching behind one of the gigantic ears. She buried her face in his matted, mangy fur. 'Mmmm, you smell lovely. Like my old comfort blanket. I think I'll call you Blanket.'

I sniffed the air. I caught the scent of old fur coat, unwashed carpet and damp dog. Nathan held his nose.

'Doesn't smell like a cof-mort blanket to me,' I whispered.

Mrs Ogg helped us to slide slowly off Blanket's side, onto the floor. The bearded driver was welcoming the others onto the coach and I joined them, leaving Daisy-May whispering goodbye to her new furry friend.

16.

As we climbed back onto the coach, I felt proud of myself. I'd helped to prevent a number of disasters and Ms Weebly was going to welcome us back to Purple Hill Primary with open arms. No emergency services. Hello end-of-year party.

I slid into a seat next to Nathan. It had been an amazing day but it was exhausting keeping 4X in order. It was good to be going home after all. The coach rumbled and moved slowly out of the car park.

Something seemed to be worrying Nathan. He pulled at my polo shirt and pointed out of the window but I couldn't see anything out there. For once, I was too tired to try to figure out what he meant. I lay my heavy head against the prickly coach seat back and wished Nathan would just speak. The coach juddered and I felt my eyelids close. I was exhausted. It was like the end of that song we'd sung on the way here, when it goes all slow and sleepy:

'We've beeeen to the zoo… zoo… zoo…' (or loo… loo… loo… depending on your choice of lyrics). Daisy-May would find that funny. She had cracked up about it on the way – hang on a minute – DAISY-MAY! I sat bolt upright in my seat, my round eyes meeting Nathan's. Nathan looked as horrified as I felt.

I checked my notebook and quickly counted heads in case she had moved seats. There should be seventeen children present. There were only sixteen.

I felt sick. We'd left Daisy-May behind.

It was that stupid mammoth. Daisy-May had been so busy stroking Blanket, she hadn't been listening to instructions. I leant across the aisle of the coach and tapped Mrs Ogg on the arm.

'Daisy-May is *missing*,' I whispered, my hand shielding my mouth. I didn't want to alarm the rest of the class; a 4X riot was not what we needed right now. Mrs Ogg's eyes met mine. They twinkled sympathetically but she raised her hands in an outward gesture as if there was nothing she could do. I'd failed. I had been so busy congratulating myself on looking after everyone that I had managed to lose one of my

best friends. This was bad. This was really bad.
A missing child would mean the police at the
very least. And for once, I wasn't worried about
Ms Weebly or the party. I was worried about
Daisy-May. The coach journey went in a blur as
I imagined how I was going to break the news to
Daisy-May's family.

WAYS TO BREAK THE NEWS TO DAISY-MAY'S FAMILY

1. Hide and let them discover it for themselves X
2. Tell them and then run away X
3. Tell them and face the fireworks

Unfortunately, it was going to have to be
option 3. I really would have to be brave this
time. As our coach drove into the school car
park I scanned the waiting crowd. I could see
my mum talking to Paige's dad, but I couldn't
see Daisy-May's parents anywhere. They were

always late.

The coach drew up near the school and we all piled out. I went to see my mum first and handed her my bag and waterproof.

'Hi love,' she said, ruffling my hair and continuing her chat with Paige's dad.

Then I saw Daisy-May's big brother, Davey-Ray, coming in through the gates. I recognised him from his wide jaw and the inky scribbles up his arms. They were like the one Daisy-May drew on my arm earlier, only I had a feeling his didn't wash off. He stood near the gates, his eyes searching the crowd.

I took a deep breath and approached him.

'It's about Daisy-May…' I said.

Davey-Ray looked bored.

'Yeah? Where is she, anyway?'

'Well… I erm…'

This was harder than I thought. What words could I possibly use to break the news?

'Spit it out, bro,' he said, taking his phone out

of the back pocket of his jeans. Then I spotted her over Davey-Ray's shoulder. Daisy-May must have come in the side entrance of the school and was squeezing through the gap between the fence and the 3N classroom. She was riding her favourite mammoth.

'Erm, nothing,' I said, 'I'll just get her.'

Davey-Ray shook his head, muttered 'weird,' and swiped his finger across the screen of his phone.

I beckoned Nathan over to join me. We ran to meet Daisy-May as she was climbing down from Blanket's back.

'I was worried,' I said. 'How did you find your way back here?'

Daisy-May grinned. She pushed up the sleeve of her school jumper to reveal the ballpoint scribbles up her arm.

'I followed you through the tunnel and then when I lost the coach I used this: it's the map of the way to the zoo. I drew it on the way there,'

she said. I exchanged smiles with Nathan.
Clever Daisy-May.

Daisy-May stood nose to trunk with Blanket.

'What are you going to do with him now?' I
asked.

Daisy-May grinned.

'Take him home, of course.'

Blanket broke wind noisily.

'What will your parents say?'

'My parents won't notice. They never notice
anything. We'll be quiet, won't we, Blanket?
And if they do notice, I'll tell them he's a dog.'

A dog. Blanket was as big as a small car and
as hairy as a highland cow.

'Come on, DM,' called Davey-Ray, looking
at his phone.

'Coming!' called Daisy-May and trotted
along beside him, stroking
Blanket's trunk as she went.
Davey-Ray didn't once unglue
his eyes from his phone.

The next day, I turned up in the classroom to find Daisy-May reading Blanket an elephant picture book in the reading corner.

'Oh no, did your parents spot him after all?' I asked her.

Daisy-May nodded.

'He kept standing in front of the TV. Silly old Blanket. Never mind. He can live here; Mrs Ogg won't mind.'

Mrs Ogg didn't mind, of course. Our first lesson was maths. We stacked the tables against the wall and sat crossed-legged on the floor. Blanket was sent outside to find pebbles, which he sucked up and deposited through the open window into a bucket. We each took a pile of pebbles and used them as counters.

'Knock knock,' said Ms Weebly, strolling in without knocking. She didn't seem to notice the baby mammoth. What was it with grown-ups round here?

'I just need to speak to your class for a moment,' she said.

Mrs Ogg didn't reply. She stayed in a cross-legged seated position on top of the teacher's desk.

'Ah, thank you,' said Ms Weebly, standing awkwardly beside her, shuffling her papers. She addressed the class.

'I wanted to inform you all that a new teacher for next year has finally been found. She must have come from a long way away because she somehow hasn't heard of this class. Which means you have another few days with Mrs – Ogg – and you will meet your new teacher on

"Meet the Teacher Day".'

There was silence for a moment. This news would take a little while to sink in. Paige put up her hand, speaking at the same time.

'Will 4X get to go to the end-of-year party, Ms Weebly?'

Ms Weebly curled her lip. 'End-of-year party?'

'Yeah,' said Mitchell. 'You said if we were good on the school trip then we get to go to the party this year.'

'Did I say that?'

I consulted my notes. That was exactly what Ms Weebly had said.

'And we were really good,' added Paige.

Ms Weebly said nothing. She turned her attention to the traffic light board.

'ALL OUR NAMES ARE ON GREEN,' said AJ.

'I can see that,' said Ms Weebly, smiling a thin-lipped smile. 'But school isn't just about behaving. Before you get to go to any party, you need to prove that you have actually learned something.'

She turned to Mrs Ogg.

'Mrs Ogg, which topic has 4X been studying this term?'

Mrs Ogg held up a book entitled *Dinosaurs and Other Prehistoric Beasts*. Ms Weebly took the book and turned the pages slowly.

'Wonderful, thank you Mrs Ogg.' Ms Weebly adjusted her glasses. 'In that case, you should be able to answer a few simple questions… I shall choose three questions from this book and if 4X can manage to answer them correctly then you shall indeed go to the ball.'

19.

This wasn't fair. She hadn't mentioned anything about any questions. But still – it was a subject that we all actually knew a bit about! Ms Weebly continued smiling. The look in her eye reminded me of yesterday's angry T-Rex.

'Question number one,' she said, reading from the book. 'What kind of water creature, with a name coming from the Greek for 'fish-lizard' resembles a dolphin with a long snout?'

An image of Ronnie in the pool played in my head. Ichthyosaur. It was an Ichthyosaur! But I didn't want to say it out loud so I kept my hand down. Paige and Georgia at the front both put up their hands. Ms Weebly waved her hand dismissively.

'Oh no, *I* will choose individuals to answer the questions.'

Mrs Weebly glanced around and her eyes settled on Daisy-May, across the room from me. Daisy-May sat with her head down, poking her thumb through the hole in the sleeve of her jumper.

'I can't remember all your names but you – child with the wild hair,' she said, pointing to Daisy-May.

'Please tell me the name of the water creature. And describe it in detail,' she added.

Daisy-May met Ms Weebly's stare with a dark scowl. She heaved herself upright and freed a marker pen from her hair. She sauntered over to the flipchart at the front of the classroom. With a few deft strokes of her pen, she drew an accurate sketch of the creature we had seen in the pool, complete with bulging eyes

and long nose. Then underneath, in curly
joined-up handwriting, she wrote,

Ichthyosaur

She sounded out each syllable clearly,
pointing with her pen. Then she returned to her
place on the carpet and collapsed back down,
looking as bored as she had done to begin with.

Ms Weebly stared between the flipchart and
the book, as if searching for mistakes.

'Even spelled correctly,' she murmured.

Ms Weebly flicked through the book for a
few seconds until she found what she was

looking for.

'Aha,' she said, 'I can see a dinosaur here called Piat-nitz-kysaurus. But there is one with an even longer name. I wonder if one of you will know it.'

Her eyes wandered around the classroom. I knew before she looked at me where they were going to settle.

'Of course. Arlo,' she said, 'I wonder if you can tell me.'

I did know a dinosaur with a really long name. Of course I did. I'd seen a group of them in real life. I suddenly felt sick and my palms were sweaty. I rubbed them up and down my trouser legs to dry them and stared at the floor.

'Micro–' I could say it perfectly in my head. I caught Ms Weebly's eye. She smiled triumphantly.

I looked at Daisy-May across the room. She couldn't help me.

'You have to say it,' whispered Ronnie, next

to me.

The seconds ticked by.

Then I heard a tapping.

Darum dum dum dum.

It was Mrs Ogg. She was drumming her fingers on the desk. Of course. I tapped my forefingers on my knee, trying to get the rhythm set in my mind. *Darum dum dum dum, tappy tap, clap clap.*

Ms Weebly sighed and turned her eyes to the ceiling.

'I'm going to have to press you for an answer,' she said.

I carried on tapping. I closed my eyes. I focused on my fingers tapping my knee as I slowly pronounced each syllable.

'Micro-pachy-cephala-saur-us.'

'Yessss!' said Mitchell, punching the air.

'GO ARLO!' said AJ and I grinned and felt as tall as an Apatasaurus.

Pink patches appeared high on Ms Weebly's

cheeks. She stopped her fake smiling and pursed her lips.

'That answer was correct,' she said. 'But you still have one more question. And this question is for… *you*.'

Ms Weebly was pointing at Nathan.

At that moment, I loathed Ms Weebly. That
was just mean. That was bullying. It was like
Reception class all over again.

'MY QUESTION IS...' Ms Weebly asked
him, speaking very loudly and slowly as if he
was stupid. Nathan was not stupid. His brain
was as big as her macaroon jar.

'...Was an Apatosaurus (a) a herbivore, (b) a
carnivore, (c) an omnivore?'

It was kind of an easy question. Easy for
most of us. Easy for Nathan, who arranged the
pebbles in front of him in the shape of an 'a'.

'I'm afraid I can only accept a verbal

answer,' said Ms Weebly, staring hard at Nathan. Nathan was never going to speak with Ms Weebly looking at him like that. With everyone looking at him and the clock tick, tick, ticking away. He only ever managed to get a word out if he was really relaxed – having a giggle. I knew that but I was sitting too far away. Luckily, someone else in the room knew that too.

Mrs Ogg had been watching Ms Weebly through narrowed eyes. Now, she jumped down from the teacher's desk and crouched behind Paige, out of Ms Weebly's eyeline. Today, Paige's hair decoration was a large, blue lacy bow. Mrs Ogg brought her mouth towards the bow, plucked it gently from Paige's head and started to chew. What was she doing?

There was silence in the classroom as one-by-one, 4X noticed what was going on. Olly pointed and giggled. Then Mitchell and Georgia and Ronnie. Then Daisy-May cracked up, followed by Nathan. Paige's confused face only added to the laughter. Paige raised up her hand to feel for the missing bow and we erupted into shrieks and giggles. Nathan's eyes had gone all crinkly and he laughed his squeaky, hissy laugh. Now was the time.

'Say it, Nathan,' I mouthed to him.

And he did. Very quietly.

'Herbivore.'

Ms Weebly saw his lips form the word. And it was loud enough for AJ, next to him, to hear.

'HERBIVORE – HE SAID HERBIVORE!'

The laughter stopped.

'That was the right answer!' cried Paige, who still hadn't figured out what was going on.

'It was right!' we all muttered, staring

expectantly at Ms Weebly.

Ms Weebly looked around at all our faces and right into the eyes of Mrs Ogg, who was grinning broadly and nodding. She knew she was beaten. She scowled and walked towards the door. Over her shoulder she muttered,

'Fine, you can go to the party… but there will be no trifle.'

The school hall didn't look like the school hall. Well it did, but the balloons and the streamers and the music made it kind of magical. Tables along one side of the hall were stacked with sausage rolls, triangular sandwiches and jugs of squash. On the other side of the hall, the black DISCO BOUNCE swayed and wobbled, lights flashing inside it.

I'm not saying that 4X behaved perfectly but we were better than before. The twins bounced up to a ledge near the top of the DISCO BOUNCE and stayed there all evening. Mitchell discovered he could stand on his head

if the floor was sticky enough. Paige and
Georgia and their lot won the dance competition
with a choreographed dance to a dinosaur song.
They even shared their sweets with us. Daisy-
May and Nathan had some of the blue ones and
spent most of the evening sticking out their
electric blue tongues.

But for me, the best bit was when AJ chanted,
'HOORAY, HOORAY, HOORAY, FOR
ARLO, NATHAN AND DAISY-MAY!' and a
group of kids lifted each of us up on their
shoulders. We bounced out of the DISCO
BOUNCE and paraded round the hall with the
other years all watching and cheering. It's funny
but I didn't think of myself as a hero. I always
thought a hero had to be loud and strong. I
didn't think I'd ever be lifted onto people's

shoulders. But here I was, and it felt good.

The best bit of the evening was also the worst bit. As I lay there, helpless, laughing and growing dizzy, I spotted a figure in the playground through the misty window. The figure had sticky-out hair and was carrying a gnarled stick. She was walking in the direction of the EXIT sign pulling her wheeled trolley. Something told me she wasn't coming back. Her eyes met mine and she smiled. I held up a hand and she held up hers in reply. Then she kept walking.

4X EX-TEACHERS

5. Mrs Ogg: July 14th: Helped us find our hidden talents. Left without saying goodbye.

After the party, there was just one week of school left. Ms Weebly was in charge again but she didn't have to do any teaching, as that week was full of special days. We had 'Dress as a Reptile Day' (iguana), 'Bring in a Random Relative Day' (Great Uncle Alan) and 'Come to School Late Day' (Ms Weebly thought of that one).

On 'Meet the Teacher Day'; we would get to meet our teacher for next year. In September, 4X would become 5 something-or-other. In Year 5 we would be nearly the oldest in the school but we weren't all that interested in having a new

teacher. Who could be better than Mrs Ogg?
Mrs Ogg believed in us. Without her, we might
as well go back to the way we were before.
Unruly, disobedient and unteachable.

When we walked into the classroom, there
was no-one there and the wall displays were
bare. The traffic light system was in its default
position, with all our names on green. Mitchell
automatically moved his own name to red as he
walked in. I took my seat.

There was a sheet of blank stickers at the
front for us to write our names. Daisy-May
wrote *Bernard* on hers. Mitchell drew a picture
of a poo. I carefully wrote out *Arlo* and stuck it
to my jumper. The noise level was high. The
twins sat cross-legged on the windowsill.
Mitchell was juggling with other people's pencil
cases.

A woman walked into the room. She was
really small – not much taller than me – with
light brown skin and long black hair swept on to

the top of her head. She wore a white dress and a summery purple scarf. She didn't say anything but gazed at the 'activity' in the room. She took in the juggling, the yelling and the baby mammoth mowing the lawn outside. She fiddled with the computer and some slow music that sounded like recorders filled the room.

She approached the twins with a 'Hi, what are your names?' and a 'Great, take a seat please.'

Her voice was soft but firm and even AJ stopped shouting to listen.

'Please join me on the carpet,' she said, and we all did. She sat on the floor with us, legs crossed.

'Hi,' she said, 'I'm Miss Pythia. I'd love one of you to tell me about your class.' Hands shot up. I hovered my hand halfway up.

'Excuse me; I can't see your name badge...' I looked up. 'Sorry – Arlo – could you please tell me a little about 4X?'

'I… er…' I coughed. 'Can I get out my notebook, please?'

'Sure.'

I took out my notebook and read aloud:

'In 4X we are unruly and bis-o, dis-ob–'

I stopped.

'Take your time.'

I clapped it out in my head.

'We are unruly and disobedient,' I read from my notebook.

Miss Pythia laughed delightedly as if I'd just said *studious and attentive*. 'Really?' she said, 'I thought that you all have hidden talents.'

'Ah, yes,' I said, and flicked a little further on in my notebook.

'Naima has a lovely singing voice. Ronnie can swim, Mitchell's a great hunter…'

'And what about you, Arlo? What's your hidden talent?'

I looked at the question marks by my name.

'Turn the page,' whispered Daisy-May.

I turned the page. There was a detailed drawing of me, juggling an Apatasaurus, a Tyrannasaurus, an Ichthyosaur and a Micropachycephalasaurus. Underneath, in familiar curly handwriting, it said:

Arlo: saving the day

I turned the book round to show Miss Pythia and she laughed.

'That sounds like a useful talent. I just know that we are going to have lots of fun next term.

Now, everyone, are there any questions you'd like to ask me?' She looked around the room and her eyes settled on Daisy-May.

'Bernard?' she invited, with a straight face.

Daisy-May looked down at her badge and smiled guiltily. 'Oh. Do you have any pets?' she said.

'A snake called Oleander and a kitten called Laurel.'

Daisy-May grinned broadly. She took a pen from her hair, whipped the sticker off her polo shirt and amended it so it read *Daisy-May*.

'Will you be staying long?' asked Mitchell. 'Most of our teachers don't stick around. Just look at Ms Weebly's notes.'

'I'll stay as long as I need to,' said Miss Pythia. She looked around the circle of children. 'And I don't have Ms Weebly's notes, but Mrs Ogg gave your class a double thumbs up.' She turned her paper around so we could see the crudely drawn thumbs.

'Do you know Mrs Ogg?' Daisy-May asked.

'Oh, I know a great many things about a great many people.'

'Can you do drumming like she did?' I asked.

Miss Pythia laughed. 'No, I'm afraid not. I have no sense of rhythm and I eat too many chocolate biscuits. Nobody's perfect. It would be a pity if we were all the same, wouldn't it?'

Miss Pythia stood and turned to the board. At the nape of her neck, under the sweep of her hair, was a strange symbol, a bit like two capital Es joined back-to-back. There was a small circle in the middle. It looked like an open eye, watching us.

Ollie took the opportunity of Miss Pythia's turned back to go back to his earlier seat by the open window. Miss Pythia didn't move but her soft voice floated over to him.

'Please remain seated on the carpet, Ollie. Danger lies by an open window,' she said.

Ollie returned to the carpet and I felt a sudden flutter in my stomach. How did she know that Ollie had moved? She hadn't even turned around. Maybe that eye really was watching us. I looked around at my classmates. Ollie raised his eyebrows in my direction but nobody else seemed to have noticed. I started a brand new page in my notebook.

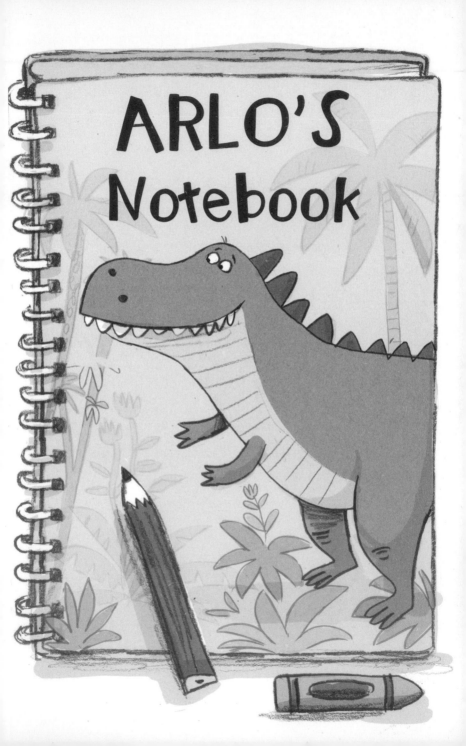

5P TEACHERS

1. <u>Miss Pythia</u>: We've just met her but I can tell that things are going to be ⌇ interesting. ⌇ She seems to know exactly what is happening without looking. Almost as if she has <u>special</u> <u>powers</u>...

MRS OGG and 4X

The end...?

Keep an eye out for
Arlo's next adventure!

ABOUT THE AUTHOR

Alice loved drawing and writing from an early age and always fancied the idea of writing a book. While working as a librarian, a website editor and an Outreach manager for a university, she always wrote for fun. It was only when she had children of her own that Alice left her full-time job and suddenly seemed to have lots of story ideas!

Alice was first published in 2013 by Maverick with her picture book *The Black and White Club* but she has since had over 30 books published in the UK and internationally, as well as writing for websites, apps and even a talking bear! Alice writes for children of all ages and, now her children have grown up, she finds herself naturally writing longer texts. Alice is fantastic at events and particularly enjoys visiting schools.

We asked Alice some very important questions:

What is the craziest thing you have done?
I do a lot of odd things when I am thinking
about stories. I once bumped into a bus stop and
recently melted my electric kettle by putting it
on the stovetop. You probably didn't mean
crazy in that way, did you?

**If you were stuck on a desert island, what
item would you want to be stranded with?**
A kettle. Preferably not electric (see above).

What's your favourite type of dinosaur?
Maiasaura – the mummy dinosaur who looked
after her babies in the nest.

If you had a super power what would it be?
I think I will choose to be able to jump into
paintings like Mary Poppins. Actually, it's a bit
like that when I write stories. I can go anywhere
I fancy.

ALO,
MRS OGG
and the
DINOSAUR ZOO

Arlo, Mrs Ogg and the Dinosaur Zoo
An original concept by author Alice Hemming
© Alice Hemming

Illustrations by Kathryn Durst
Represented by The Bright Agency
www.thebrightagency.com

Published by MAVERICK ARTS PUBLISHING LTD
Studio 3a, City Business Centre, 6 Brighton Road,
Horsham, West Sussex, RH13 5BB
+44 (0) 1403 256941
© Maverick Arts Publishing Limited April 2018

A CIP catalogue record for this book is available
at the British Library.

ISBN: 978-1-84886-320-0